S0-ANG-346

CHILDREN'S ROOM
Public Library
South Bend, Indiana

The
Easter Surprise

by Janet McDonnell
illustrated by Linda Hohag

created by Wing Park Publishers

Ⓟ CHILDRENS PRESS®

CHICAGO

PUBLIC LIBRARY
FEB 24 1994
SOUTH BEND, INDIANA

Library of Congress Cataloging-in-Publication Data

McDonnell, Janet, 1962-
 The Easter surprise / by Janet McDonnell ; illustrated by
Linda Hohag.
  p.   cm. — (Circle the year with holidays)
 "Created by Wing Park Publishers."
 Summary: Julie celebrates Easter by receiving a basket of
candy, going to church, and enjoying an Easter egg hunt.
Includes instructions for Easter crafts and games.
 ISBN 0-516-00683-5
 [1. Easter—Fiction.] I. Hohag, Linda, ill. II. Title.
III. Series.
PZ7.M478436Eas   1993
[E]—dc20   93-11004
                                                   CIP
                                                    AC

Copyright ©1993 by Childrens Press, Inc.
All rights reserved. Printed simultaneously in Canada.
Printed in the United States of America.
1 2 3 4 5 6 7 8 9 10 11 12 R 99 98 97 96 95 94 93

EASY   LA SALLE
McDonnell, Janet
The Easter surprise

The
Easter Surprise

This is the house were Julie lives with her
mother, her father, her brother, Ben, and her
cat, Sadie. One cool, clear day in spring,
exciting things were happening both outside
and inside Julie's house.

Outside, bright green buds were unfolding on the trees. Birds were building nests to get ready for the eggs they would lay.

Inside, Julie and her family were busy getting ready for a very special holiday.

The kitchen table was crowded with glasses of pink, purple, green, and yellow dye. The middle of the table was filling up with brightly-colored eggs.

"Do you think this will be enough for tomorrow?" asked Julie.

Her mother laughed. "I sure hope so," she
said.

Julie was so excited. She loved Easter, and
coloring eggs was one of her favorite parts of
the holiday.

As she lifted a pink egg out of some dye, she began to wonder. "Why do we color eggs at Easter?" she asked.

"Eggs remind us of new life," said her father. "And Easter is a celebration of new life."

"Like the baby chicks that come from eggs?"
asked Julie.

"Yes, and another kind of new life too," said
her father.

"Like what?" asked Julie.

"You'll see," said her father.

That night, before going to bed, Julie put out the pretty clothes that she would wear to church in the morning. As she climbed into bed, she had a silly idea.

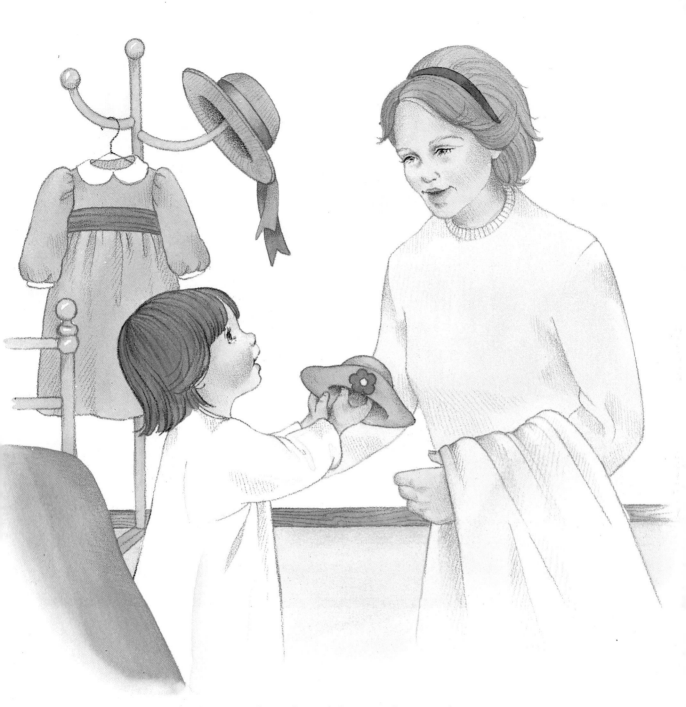

"Maybe Sadie should get dressed up too."
She pulled off her doll's hat. "This would be
a perfect Easter bonnet for her. SADIE!" she
called.

But the cat did not come. Julie looked under the bed.

"Where could she be, Mom?"

"Oh, you know Sadie," said her mother. "She's probably hiding somewhere. We'll find her in the morning." With that, she kissed Julie good night and turned off the lights.

The next morning, Easter morning, Julie and
Ben ran down the stairs in excitement. "Happy
Easter!" they cried.

"Happy Easter!" said their father. "Look what
the Easter Bunny brought you!"

On the kitchen table were two big baskets filled with jelly beans, chocolate eggs, and all kinds of goodies. Julie wanted to taste everything right away, but her mom did not think that was a good idea.

"You can have one chocolate egg after breakfast. Save the rest for later," she said.

Then Julie noticed a fuzzy, toy chick in the middle of her basket. "Oh, Sadie will love this!" she said. "Where is Sadie?"

"I'm sure she'll turn up," said her father. "But we don't have time to hunt for her now. We'll find her when we get home from church."

In church, Julie looked around at the
beautiful Easter lilies. But she stopped looking
around and listened when the minister told
the story of why Christians celebrate Easter.

He told of how Jesus died long, long ago, and how sad the people were. Three days later, some of Jesus' friends went to the place where Jesus was buried. The Bible says that an angel appeared and said that Jesus had risen.

"And that is why today is such a joyful holiday for Christians," said the minister. Then the choir sang a beautiful song. Julie thought her mother's voice was the prettiest of all.

After church, Julie's relatives all came over
for the Easter celebration.

Julie's cousin Scott loved cats. Before he was
even out of the car, he was asking, "Where's
Sadie? Where's Sadie?"

"That's a good question," said Julie. "Where is my cat?"

They began to look all over for Sadie, but no luck. Soon Julie's mother was ringing the bell.

"Time to eat!" she called.

Julie's family sat around the long table to begin their Easter feast. The ham was delicious, but Julie didn't feel much like eating. She was worried about Sadie.

When the dishes were all cleared away,
Julie's mom said, "Now let's start the Easter
egg hunt!"

"Good. I'll hunt for Sadie while I hunt for
eggs," Julie said to herself.

Julie looked in the flower pot. She looked under the bushes. But she saw no eggs and no Sadie. Then she looked in the mailbox.

"What's this?" she said. There was a pink and purple egg. Under it was a note. It said:
"Follow the arrows and open your eyes, and you will get a big surprise.
Love,
The Easter Bunny"

Julie looked down and saw an arrow made
out of jelly beans. Then she found another,
and another. She followed them all the way
to the barn.

Julie opened the door and peeked inside.
She couldn't believe her eyes! There in the
corner, on an old blanket, was Sadie. And next
to her were five tiny kittens!

"Sadie! You're a mommy!" cried Julie.

Everyone came to see what Julie had found.

"Well, well," said her father. "What an Easter surprise."

"It's the best one I've ever had" said Julie.

Julie leaned down to the soft, furry kittens. "Happy Easter," she whispered.

MAKE YOUR OWN EASTER FUN

You don't have to wait for the Easter Bunny to bring you a basket. You can make your own! It's easy!

You will need:
- a plastic coated paper plate (you may want to use a plate with a spring pattern on it, like daisies!)
- an empty, two-pound coffee can
- a large thick rubber band
- warm water (not hot)
- a long strip of heavy construction paper (about 2 inches wide, 18 inches long)
- two fasteners

What to do:

1. Dip the paper plate in the water. Make sure it gets completely wet.

2. Place the plate over the top or bottom (preferably bottom) of a coffee can as shown. Try to center the plate over the can. Press the edges of the plate down around the coffee can. Put the rubber band around the plate to keep it in place.

3. Let the plate dry completely. This should take about four hours. Take off the rubber band and remove the plate. It should stay in the shape of the bottom of the can.

4. Attach the strip of construction paper to the plate with the fasteners to make a handle. (You may want to decorate the handle first with crayons, markers, or paint!) Now you can fill your basket with grass, jelly beans, and other Easter goodies!

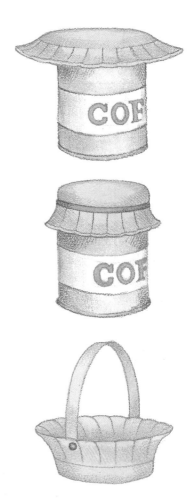

Funny Bunny Face

This bunny is not for eating, but his face is made from a plate and spoons!

You will need:
- one white paper plate
- two white plastic spoons
- white or pink construction paper
- permanent black marker
- crayons
- pencil
- scissors

What to do:

1. Place the two spoons side by side in the middle of the plate. With a pencil, make a mark just under the bowls of each spoon, and a mark a little ways up (about 1/2") from the ends of the spoons.

2. Cut a small slit with scissors at each mark. (Ask an adult to help you with this.)

3. Slide the spoons through the slits as shown. The curved parts of the spoons will be the eyes, and the ends of the handles will be the teeth!

4. Now decorate your funny bunny. Using a permanent marker, make eyeballs in the spoons. Use crayons to draw a nose, mouth, and whiskers. Then cut out ears from the construction paper. Glue them from the back of the plate.

An Edible Easter Bunny!

Surprise your friends with this adorable bunny salad. This recipe makes two servings.

You will need:

1 small can of pears
4 lettuce leaves
4 blanched almonds
4 raisins
1 maraschino cherry
½ cup of shredded coconut

What to do:

1. Tear the lettuce leaves into small pieces. Arrange them on two small plates.

2. Place half a pear on each plate on top of the lettuce, as shown.

3. Now make the bunny faces! For each bunny, use two raisins for the eyes, two almonds for the ears, and half a cherry for the nose.

4. Finish your bunnies with a little pile of coconut for each tail.

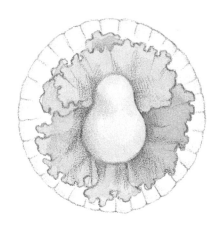

Egg-sellent Easter Games!

There are lots of fun games to play with Easter eggs. Here are a few ideas. Can you make up your own Easter egg game?

The Egg Roll

Find a grassy hill outside, or make a hill by using a board or heavy piece of cardboard as a ramp. Each player takes a turn rolling his or her egg down the ramp. The one that rolls the farthest wins.

The Spoon Race

Mark a start line and a finish line. Racers must carry their eggs on a spoon to the finish line. They may not touch the eggs with their hands.

The Nose Nudging Race

Once again, mark a start and finish line. Racers begin with their eggs on the floor. They must push the eggs to the finish line with their noses only.

The Egg Roll

The Spoon Race

The Nose Nudging Race

31

j EASY
McDonnell, Janet   LA SALLE
The Easter surprise

WITHDRAWN
from St. Joseph County Public Library
Excess____V____Damaged_____
Date___8-13___Initials_____